Terror in the Towers

Amazing stories from the World Trade Center disaster

by Adrian Kerson
with photographs

A Bullseye Nonfiction Book

Random House 🏠 New York

To J.D., who made it all happen

Text copyright © 1993 by Sydelle Kramer
All rights reserved under International and Pan-American Copyright Conventions.
Published in the United States by Random House, Inc., New York, and simultaneously
in Canada by Random House of Canada Limited, Toronto.

Cover design by Michaelis/Carpelis Design Associates, Inc.

Photo on page 4 courtesy of UPI/Bettmann.

Library of Congress Cataloging-in-Publication Data
Kerson, Adrian.
Terror in the towers : amazing stories from the World Trade Center disaster /
by Adrian Kerson.
    p. cm.
"Bullseye books."
"A Read it to believe it book."
Includes bibliographical references and index.
ISBN 0-679-85332-4 (pbk.)—ISBN 0-679-95332-9 (lib. bdg.)
1. World Trade Center Bombing, New York, N.Y., 1993—Juvenile literature.
2. Terrorism—New York (N.Y.)—Juvenile literature.
I. Title.
HV6432.K47 1993
364.1'09747'1—dc20
93-10661

Manufactured in the United States of America 10 9 8 7 6 5 4 3 2 1

Contents

1. The Blast   5

2. No Way Out   13

3. Trapped   21

4. Help Arrives   26

5. Fighting for Life   37

6. In the Dark   47

7. Gasping for Air   57

8. Out of a Nightmare   63

9. The Great Escape   73

10. When the Smoke Clears   84

To Find Out More   92

Acknowledgments   94

Index   95

Chapter 1

The Blast

February 26, 1993. It is an ordinary day in New York City. Outside, snow is falling lightly, and the temperature is a chilly twenty-seven degrees. But at the World Trade Center, no one's thinking about the weather. The nearly fifty-five thousand people who work there can't wait for the day to end. It's lunchtime on Friday, and everyone is looking forward to the weekend.

Thousands of other people are also in the Trade Center. Some are there on business. Others have come to shop or eat in the busy downstairs mall. Many are staying at the Vista Hotel, one of seven buildings in the Center. A few are in an underground station, waiting for a train to New Jersey.

Crowds of tourists are at the Trade Center to visit the Twin Towers. These 110-floor office buildings are the Trade Center's stars. At 1,350 feet—more than a quarter mile high—they're the world's second tallest buildings. Only the Sears Tower in Chicago is higher.

One tower has an indoor observation deck on the 107th floor. Its roof has an outdoor viewing platform also—the highest anywhere. From either spot, people can see as far as fifty-five miles on a clear day.

There's a huge garage under the Trade Center. A yellow Ford van has been parked there for less than an hour. It's among two thousand other cars in the garage, including a fleet used by the U.S. Secret Service.

Yet none of these cars is like the yellow van.

Packed inside it are a number of cardboard boxes. The boxes look completely harmless— but together they hold about twelve hundred pounds of explosives.

The yellow van is hiding a gigantic bomb!

The World Trade Center garage is made up of four floors, all underground. The van is parked on B-2, the second level going down, on the ramp to the floor above. It is directly below the Vista Hotel, with the Twin Towers on either side.

At exactly 12:18 P.M., the yellow van explodes. The bomb blows it into little metal pieces. At the same time, a scorching ball of fire shoots through the air. The explosion's force moves in a wave as fast as twenty thousand feet per second.

Every building for a mile around shakes. Thousands hear a boom, but no one is sure exactly what it is.

In the garage, the bomb carves out a deep

crater. It's as wide as two hundred feet in places and more than five stories deep. Thousands of pounds of rubble smash into the pit. At the bottom lie huge chunks of concrete and whole cinder blocks. They look as though they've been tossed there like pebbles.

Solid concrete walls are shot through with big holes. Ceilings over two feet thick crumble like cookies. Pipes break open, and nearly two million gallons of water burst out. Parts of the garage become flooded with a foot and a half of water.

Steam pipes snap, and boiling mist hisses out. Gas pipelines dangle dangerously. Electrical wires swing free like ropes. Guardrails are ripped out as though they are toothpicks.

Steel bars bend, garage ramps buckle. Doors fold up like pieces of paper. The dust is so thick it's like a sandstorm. Soon a layer of soot covers everything.

Cars explode and then burn down to metal.

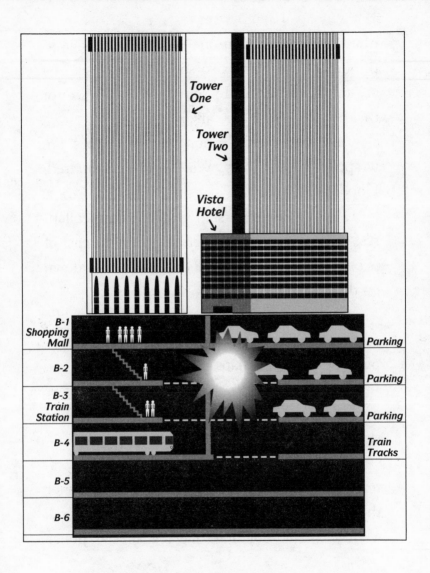

Many are tossed from one end of the garage to the other. The blast is so strong that other cars are totally flattened. In some places, it's so hot that paint peels off the cars instantly.

Cars are twisted around pillars. Pipes are wrapped around cars. Windows are shattered. Hoods are blown off.

Down in the train station, the ceiling collapses. A hailstorm of concrete pelts dozens of people on the platform. Cinder blocks rain down on the escalators.

In the hotel above, the lobby crumples like a soda can. The floor of the ballroom cracks. A piece of the ceiling flaps down.

The Twin Towers tremble. Lobby windows explode. Marble slabs crash off the walls. Smoke slithers up the buildings.

Inside the towers, all communications systems are destroyed. There is a command center that runs everything—but nothing in it works anymore. The buildings have a special police force—but their telephones are dead. There is so much confusion that the only prisoner escapes.

Power lines are down. The public-address system has blown up. All the closed-circuit television monitors are broken. Many of the city's TV stations have lost the power to broadcast because their antennas stand on top of the Twin Towers.

The buildings have fans to keep the air inside fresh and clean. But every one of them has stopped whirring. There's nothing to clear the smoke that is now swirling up through the floors.

The towers have a second power system in case the main one breaks down. But the bomb has destroyed both of them completely. So no alarms go off to warn people to get out.

All over the city, rescue workers get emergency calls. More than 150 ambulances rush toward the Twin Towers. Police cars speed downtown with sirens screaming. Soon FBI agents and Red Cross volunteers hurry over.

The bomb has caused a sixteen-alarm fire. One hundred fire trucks dash toward the World Trade Center. Seven hundred and fifty firefighters are on their way.

Nearly one hundred thousand people are trapped inside the buildings.

Chapter 2

No Way Out

It's 12:18. Three Secret Service agents have just parked their car in the Trade Center's garage. They start toward the exit. All of a sudden, there is a tremendous blast. It's so loud agent Brenda Russillo thinks she'll never hear again. It's so strong it knocks her out of her high heels.

She flies fifteen feet through the air and lands on her chest. She throws her coat over her head to protect herself from falling debris. There's no doubt in her mind—a bomb has just gone off.

A small section of the huge crater dug by the bomb blast—the hole was over 200 feet wide and several stories deep. (Reuters/Bettmann)

The explosion hurls the second agent twenty feet away. His eye is cut. So is his face. He crawls close to Brenda. She has cuts up and down her legs.

At first the third agent thinks someone has knocked him to the ground. But he quickly realizes what's actually happened. His face bleeding, he hollers for the other two.

The garage is completely dark. It's filling fast with smoke. What if there's a second explosion? The Secret Service agents know they have to get out.

But most of the people who are caught in the Trade Center are confused about what to do. Some think there's been an earthquake or an electrical explosion. On the fifty-fifth floor of one of the towers, most believe a helicopter has crashed into the building.

Many people go right back to work. But near the garage, in the basement offices, men and women are fighting for their lives.

At 12:18, Vito DeLeo is on level B-2 of the basement. Vito helps run machines to keep the towers' air cool and fresh. In huge buildings like these, the windows don't open. He's eating lunch at his desk when a flash of light races toward him. He doesn't know what it is—he's never seen anything like it.

Before he can move, his desk rears up like a horse. The ceiling collapses, the walls tumble in.

His desk falls down over his body. But Vito is lucky. The desk protects him from the hail of debris.

Scrunched down under it, Vito feels warm blood on his face. It's pitch-black in the room. He wonders if he's dead.

One level higher, on B-1, secretary Joann Hilton is planning her weekend. But suddenly there's a terrific boom, and the lights start to fade. The ceiling collapses. As if she's sitting in quicksand, her chair begins sinking into the floor.

Soon the room is black. She's stuck in her chair in the floor. She feels as though she's trapped in a cave.

Joseph Cacciatore, a mechanic, is stunned by the blast. He'd just glanced at the clock in the basement cafeteria when his contact lenses were blown out of his eyes. The heat of a fire seems to be cooking his body. His eye socket shatters. Blood runs in streams down his face.

People are shouting for help all around Joseph. But he can't see a thing—not even a flicker of light.

Hundreds of people in the basement are hurt. Some are completely buried under debris. Those who can move try to help the injured.

A few find flashlights and lead an escape. Others break down locked exit doors and search for some way out. Some are groaning. Many are bleeding. A cafeteria has been destroyed, and forty people are trapped inside.

There's fear in the basement. There's terrible pain. But no one is abandoned. People stick together.

In the mall on level B-1, there are many shoppers at 12:18. The stores are crowded with workers on their lunch breaks. Rose Kessler is in Woolworth's. She's just had her hair done in Tower One. Suddenly there's a bang, and smoke gushes through the air.

Around her, people start to run. They're one

floor below the street. But Rose is eighty-eight years old—she walks. Her hands begin to shake. Somehow she knows a bomb has gone off.

Meanwhile Joyce Reynolds has left her office at the part of the Trade Center called the Commodities Exchange. She's four blocks away eating pasta when the restaurant shakes. The lights fade, then burn bright. Everyone wonders what has happened.

Dan Leach doesn't have time to go out to lunch. He also works in the Commodities Exchange—right next door to the gigantic Twin Towers.

Dan is in a room with two thousand other people. No matter what happens, he doesn't like to be disturbed. But at 12:18, he hears a pop and the building trembles. Around him two thousand people cry "Whoa!" all at once.

The computers go dead, but then the screens relight. Dan is relieved. He can keep working.

High in the tall towers, there's total confusion. Arda Nazerian is at a meeting on the fifty-seventh floor of Tower Two. She has an exciting job—she works for the governor of New York. When the building shivers at 12:18, Arda thinks a bolt of lightning has struck it.

No one in her office stops working—until they smell smoke. Soon someone spots it spurting out of vents near the windows. Now everyone knows something is wrong.

Arda is scared. She grabs her coat and handbag. Then she and her coworkers head down the stairs. Still, she tells herself, she'll be back at work in a little while. She keeps waiting for someone to yell "False alarm!"

Accountant Geralyn Hearne is in the cafeteria on the forty-third floor, eating a salad. Suddenly the room goes dark. Smoke starts making her sick. She's almost seven months pregnant. What if breathing in the smoke hurts her baby?

Her friend Donna Anderson rushes her into the hall. Desperately they hunt for someplace less smoky. On the forty-fourth floor, the mail-room looks clear. They feel relieved—but then something terrible happens.

Geralyn is seized by a terrible attack of illness. Her arms and legs jerk violently. She has trouble breathing. Donna is afraid her friend is about to die.

All over the towers, people are frightened. They ask each other, What's going on? The only thing they're sure of is that smoke is everywhere. It's surging like a flood through halls and stairways and offices. It's traveled from the basement all the way to the 110th floor.

No alarms have gone off. There have been no announcements. Most people do not panic. Still, their instinct is to escape. But should they go downstairs or remain where they are?

The smoke is starting to choke them. Will it be easier to breathe on the ground? Or if they descend, will they walk straight into the fire?

Chapter 3

Trapped

At 12:18, Joseph Gibney is talking on the phone. He's finishing up his lunch—a slice of pizza. Joseph is a lawyer who must use a wheelchair. His office is on the thirty-seventh floor.

Suddenly there's a roar and a quaking. Everything jiggles around him. Before he knows what to think, the phone goes dead.

Deborah Matut is watching TV on the 110th floor. She works for a television station and makes sure its picture and sound are perfect. She's doing her job when the explosion occurs.

Black smoke slowly fills the hallway. She runs to the office door and slams it shut. Through the peephole, she watches smoke creeping everywhere. It begins to ooze silently into the room.

Deborah has asthma—an illness that sometimes makes it hard to breathe. She's also pregnant. She knows it's dangerous to panic, but she can't help feeling scared.

A coworker tells her to plug up the door. The office sink doesn't work, so she wets paper towels with bottled water. If she can stuff them into the cracks around the doorway, the smoke will take longer to seep into the room.

Down on the eighteenth floor, editor Michael Santoli's racing against a deadline. He's got until 1:00 to get his work to the printer. Suddenly there's a noise like thunder. The building lurches forward just once. All the fans stop running. The office has never been so quiet.

It's 12:18. Only forty-two minutes to deadline. Michael goes right back to work.

On the fifty-seventh floor, lawyer Jane Welsh is on the phone. All at once, she hears a strange kind of bang. The building quivers, then steadies. The lights go out, then come back on.

The public-address system doesn't broadcast a warning. It's as though nothing has happened. But then Jane smells smoke. "I've got to get out!" she thinks. "Whatever this thing is, it's not going to get me."

She grabs her coat and briefcase and quickly changes into her boots. Her eyeglasses are stuck firmly in her short red hair.

The only way out is the staircase. She's not going to let herself get stuck in an elevator. If there's a fire, smoke and flames can trap her inside.

The staircase is jammed. Jane hates crowds, but she plunges in. A man yells, "This is only a drill," but she doesn't believe him. She's absolutely sure this is the real thing.

Not everyone is lucky enough to be able to

reach the stairs. When the bomb goes off, hundreds of people are riding in the huge elevators. The most crowded car is filled with seventy-two people. Inside are seventeen kindergartners, a third-grade class, and a class of fifth graders. There are also teachers, parents, other adults, and the elevator operator.

At 12:18, the elevator bumps to a halt. It's just below the thirty-second floor. The lights go out. Some of the children scream. The car is as dark as the inside of a coffin. Smoke slowly drifts in—no one knows what's happening. Will the car stay where it is—or plunge to the ground?

Forty-four other elevators have also stopped. The people inside them are trapped. But inside a car stopped on the fifty-eighth floor, one man believes there may be a way to escape. Eugene Fasullo thinks he can break out of the car. He is an engineer who helped build the Twin Towers. No one knows the buildings better than he does.

Seven other people are with Eugene. He tells

them the walls are made of thin material. Together they decide to dig their way out.

Smoke is flowing into the elevator. There's no time to lose. They grab keys, nail files—whatever they can find. They'll use those, plus their fingers and nails, to try and claw their way through the wall.

The clock ticks on. The fire burns below.

By now most people realize they're in deep trouble. But few push or shove. No one screams, "Get out of my way!" They're all in this together.

Chapter 4

Help Arrives

At 12:21, the first firefighters appear. Four minutes later, the first ambulance drives up. It doesn't matter that it's freezing. It doesn't matter that snow is falling. Rescue workers are trained to come quickly.

They don't waste any time starting their jobs. By 12:26, the Vista Hotel is emptied. All traffic is halted by 12:30. The police have cleared the streets for one of the biggest rescue operations ever.

When fireman Kevin Shea arrives, he's told

An injured man is helped from the Trade Center by two rescue workers. (AP/Wide World Photos)

that people are trapped in the basement. He and his company, Rescue Unit 1, quickly run downstairs. They begin a careful search for anyone who's injured.

27

Suddenly their lieutenant stops them. He's heard a cry for help. Kevin leads the men in single file as they try to find where the cry came from. "Help! Help!" a man's voice shouts. Now all the firefighters hear him.

Kevin calls out to the buried man. He wants him to know that help is on the way. It's dark and it's smoky. The ceiling is caving in. Kevin turns to warn his comrades about falling concrete.

But before he can say a word, the floor collapses beneath him. Down, down he falls. He completely disappears. The men in his unit don't know if he's dead or alive.

Meanwhile, in the Commodities Exchange, everything is work as usual. Dan Leach gets up from his computer and goes to the bathroom. But something strange is going on in there—the men are staring out the windows.

What could they all be watching? Dan is curious—he looks out too. Then he sees it. Smoke is churning out of Tower One.

But he's too busy to worry. What can smoke in the tower do to him in the Exchange? "It's no big deal," he thinks. He goes back to work.

In the garage, Brenda Russillo and her fellow Secret Service agents decide they'll be safer in a car. Besides, the best way out of the garage is to drive to an exit. There's only one problem— where *is* their car?

They begin to search, but they can barely see. The smoke is so heavy now they can hardly breathe. Every car they pass is crushed. If they find theirs, will it even start?

They spot it at last, but the roof is dented. Every one of the windows is shattered. Yet—to their amazement—the engine is fine. The car's ready to go! In an instant, the two men jump into their seats.

Brenda can see that the car is full of glass. But she knows she has no choice. She settles into a seat of sharp slivers.

Another car has been blown in front of theirs.

They maneuver around it and start on their way. But even with the headlights on, the garage is as dark as a grave. There's only one way for the agent to drive—from memory. Luckily he's been here many times before.

Somehow they reach the other side of the garage. All three leap from the car and race up the stairs. Out on the street, they stand in the snow and cough and cough. Brenda is freezing— her feet are bare.

All around them, more rescue workers are rushing in. Deputy Chief Paul Maniscalco of the Emergency Medical Service (EMS) is there. He watches smoke billow from the towers, steam spout from the ground. People are staggering out of every exit in the buildings.

They're crying, they're limping, they're gasping for breath. When they cough, they spit out black phlegm. When they wipe their noses, the mucus is black. They're as filthy as if they'd rolled in giant ashtrays.

Paul quickly realizes that thousands of people will need help. Emergency vehicles as large as school buses are already speeding to the Trade Center. He makes plans to use city buses as temporary shelters. That way the injured can rest out of the cold.

By 12:30 P.M., Lieutenant Dan Loeb of Engine Company 34 has arrived. He and his men run into Tower One's lobby. The ceiling of the lobby is six stories high. The whole place is dense with smoke.

Streams of people are coming down the stairs. Dan and his men charge up to keep the crowd moving smoothly.

Dan has his helmet on, and his heavy boots and uniform. He's carrying a walkie-talkie and a big flashlight. He doesn't know what's ahead, but he has to do his job. No matter how he feels, he must appear confident. If a fireman looks afraid, that will only frighten people.

Still, he can't help worrying about his wife,

Rescue vehicles crowded the streets around the Trade Center just minutes after the explosion.
(Donna Dietrich/Newsday)

Marilyn. She works in the other tower—he wishes he could look for her. Yet he knows he has to stay right here, no matter what. There are hundreds of people around him who need his help.

Marilyn Loeb is safe. She's in Tower Two's lobby. The air is full of smoke, yet she doesn't want to go out in the cold. Finally she has to flee.

From the street, she sees a black cloud rolling out of the Vista Hotel. There are policemen on the sidewalk overcome by smoke. She doesn't know what's going on, but she stays close to the tower. She's going to wait outside and make sure her coworkers get out.

In the mall just below, eighty-eight-year-old Rose Kessler keeps on walking. She may be slow, but she knows she's going to make it. She feels the spirit of her dead husband guiding her out of the building.

Down in the basement on level B-2, rescue workers stumble on a horrible sight. Four friends eating together have died in their office. Their names are William Macko, Robert Kirkpatrick, Monica Smith, and Steven Knapp.

The walls and ceiling collapsed on them. Three were killed by a fourteen-thousand-pound steel beam.

Not far away, Vito DeLeo squirms out from under his desk. Crawling on all fours, he manages to get out of his office. Somehow he feels his way up the stairs.

He can't see where he's going. The smoke makes it hard to breathe. But all at once, there's light ahead—it's the street!

Joann Hilton is still stuck in her chair in the floor. Suddenly there are hands and arms around her body. Someone wrenches her out of the ground.

She's free! But there's no time for real thanks. She and her coworkers just hurry out of there.

In the basement cafeteria, Joseph Cacciatore feels the fire getting closer. His skin is so hot it's as though he's burning up. He's trapped in a smoky darkness gloomier than a foggy night.

Somehow he finds a water valve and turns it on. Water sprays all over him. At last he's cool. The fire hisses and spits—but it won't burn him now.

Hundreds of feet above, Jane Welsh still has her eyeglasses stuck in her hair. Right now she doesn't think the smoke on the stairs is too bad. But the farther down she goes, the thicker it gets. Is she heading the right way? Or is she moving toward the fire?

Near her one woman cries and prays. A man in shirtsleeves clutches his lunch. It gets darker and darker. Should she go back up? She grits her teeth and keeps descending the stairs.

In Tower Two, Arda Nazerian feels her way through the gloom. On the staircase, people yell "Does anyone have a light?" Here and there, people pull out small penlights. Thin beams flash out and briefly brighten the steps.

From each tower floor, more people flood onto the stairs. Everyone seems to be watching out for each other. Whenever there is crowding or people moving too fast, the word goes out: "Slow down!"

The smoke gets denser. It's so dark Arda clings to the railing. To keep her balance, she slides her hand along the wall. When will this be over? When will she get down?

Chapter 5

Fighting for Life

Down in the basement, fireman Kevin Shea has fallen forty-five feet. It's as though he's jumped off the top of a four-story building. He hits the ground feet first, then smashes onto his knees. His helmet stays on his head but his face smacks into a wall.

At first Kevin doesn't move. He's in terrible pain. His nose is broken, and so are both his feet. Part of his forehead is crushed, and his left kneecap is cracked. His right ankle is broken, and he has sprains and strains everywhere.

He knows he's lucky to be alive.

There are flames to his left. Rushing water surges over him. He's surrounded by metal bars that stab the air like spears. Heavy cinder blocks crash nearby—if one hits him, he might be killed.

An avalanche of concrete is strewn on the ground. He suddenly realizes what's happened— he's tumbled into the bomb crater!

Off comes his mask. He shouts for help. He knows he's got to get out of here. He must try to move.

Strapped around his wrist is his heavy flashlight. He takes it off and places it carefully beside him.

Then a cinder block flies down out of the darkness. Slam! It shatters his flashlight. What a close call! He can only think, "I'm a lucky man."

But the flames are moving closer. He can feel their burning heat. He's a fireman—there's got to be some way he can protect himself. Nearby is a big panel that's been ripped out of the wall. He drags it over his body.

The water gushing over him slaps up against the panel. It makes a huge spray that showers down on the fire. The flames dart away. He's safe for the moment.

Then Kevin shouts for help. Over his radio, he hollers the code word used by people in trouble, "Mayday! Mayday!"

But no one answers.

High above Kevin, on the eighteenth floor, Michael Santoli gives up on his deadline. Someone's just told him that the lobby is filling with smoke. He knows he has to leave. He grabs his coat and a cup of clam chowder he ordered in for lunch.

When he reaches the staircase, it's jammed with people. Everyone is trying to leave. There are ten steps to a flight, two flights to a floor. The crowd is moving so slowly it takes five minutes to walk the twenty steps from one floor to the next.

Michael holds his chowder firmly. When he finally gets outside, at least he'll have something to eat.

Joseph Gibney isn't thinking about the cold. Two friends, Jack and Andy, have lifted him from his wheelchair. They head down the stairs, carrying him on their shoulders. It's hard work—Jack and Andy are dripping with sweat.

The smoke gets heavier the lower they go. Andy is exhausted—he can't go on anymore. Joseph knows Andy must rest. He doesn't expect Jack to carry him alone.

None of the men know what to do.

On the forty-fourth floor, Geralyn Hearne is very sick. But a fireman has found her. He knows she needs help quickly. He carries her in a chair to the thirty-fourth floor. Geralyn's friend Donna stays close behind.

All the way down, the two women hear

screaming. People trapped in elevators are yelling for help.

In the schoolchildren's car, some of the kindergartners are sobbing. "I want my mommy," a few of them cry. Two are so terrified they throw up. The teachers decide to ask everyone to sing. They hope that will pass the time and keep the children calm. Soon seventy-two voices begin to belt out songs. They sing the theme to a favorite television program, and "John Jacob Jingleheimer Schmidt."

No one in the elevator moves. They're afraid any sudden motion will make the car fall.

On the 107th floor, more schoolchildren line the observation deck. Three second-grade classes stare out at the city below. But the deck is growing cloudy with smoke.

Guards tell the teachers to head to the roof. It's no longer safe to be on the deck. They take the children up and then out of the building. Standing above the 110th floor, they feel as though they're at the top of the world.

At first, it's a great adventure. There's a crowd of people on the roof. They join up with a class of kindergartners. But then the children start to feel cold. Soon they're scared. Some are crying.

The teachers have a good idea. Everyone will share clothing. Children who have both hats and hoods will lend their hats to those who need one. Whoever has no gloves will borrow one from a child with two. Then both children will keep their bare hand in their pockets.

In a little while, the classes feel better. They do exercises to warm up. They even sing their favorite songs.

Suddenly they hear a whoosh and a great roar. A blue and white police helicopter is directly overhead.

New York City police sergeant Timothy Farrell is aboard. He looks down from the helicopter onto the roof of the second tower.

A rescue helicopter hovers over Tower Two.
(Anthony Fioranelli)

Through the snow, he sees nearly two hundred people waving at him.

But the roof of the other tower is completely empty. Timothy knows that means people are locked inside. Those on the second tower's roof might be cold. But inside the first, they might be dying.

The helicopter circles the roof of Tower One. It's impossible to land—there are antennas and lights in the way. Timothy is going to have to reach the roof by rope.

The helicopter doesn't budge. The pilot keeps it still in the sky. Its propellers churn the air noisily. Timothy puts on his helmet, then slips on his gloves. He doesn't want to cut his hands when he slides down the rope.

He hooks the rope on to the helicopter and throws it down toward the roof. It dangles below him, through the snowy mist. Then he gets into a harness that clips on to the rope. That way he can't fall off no matter what happens.

It's past 1:00 P.M. when Timothy steps out of the helicopter. The rope rushes through his hands as he slides fifty feet down. With thick clouds all around him, he lands with his knees bent.

The draft from the helicopter makes it hard for him to stand. Snow bites at his face, then quickly melts. But he's made it! He's standing on the top of the tower.

The roof door is locked. He was right—people *are* trapped below. He breaks the door open and races inside.

Deborah Matut has plugged all the cracks around her door. Suddenly it flies open—there's a policeman in her doorway! Timothy wants everyone in her office to get out onto the roof. It's 1:30, and her floor is very smoky. She and her coworkers need to breathe some fresh air.

She grabs her coat and gloves and runs into the hallway. It's so dark out there it's as though she's stepped into a closet. She keeps her hands on the walls as she feels her way down the hall. At last she can see some light.

She runs up some stairs and out into the day. It doesn't matter that it's windy, it doesn't matter that it's cold, it doesn't matter that it's snowing—there's clean, fresh air!

She coughs and coughs. She can hardly see. She's dirty and rumpled—but she's alive!

Chapter 6

In the Dark

In front of the Twin Towers, emergency vehicles are still pulling up. Rescue workers run back and forth carrying oxygen tanks and stretchers. Everywhere the street is full of noise and movement.

Yet one part of the World Trade Center seems very quiet. The Commodities Exchange is almost empty now. It's past 1:30 P.M.—the building has been evacuated.

But Joyce Reynolds and a coworker named Sandy are heading back inside. Their lunch had been interrupted by a phone call about the explosion. The caller said that everyone was leaving the Commodities Exchange, but that people could return to the building to pick up their belongings.

The women get into an elevator. The car begins to rise. Suddenly the lights go out. The car stops abruptly.

They're trapped just above the second floor. Sandy pounds on every button. It's so dark she and Joyce can't even see each other.

Then they hear voices. They start yelling for help. They bang and bang on the door. But nobody hears them.

Joyce takes off her coat and sits on it like a pillow. Sandy keeps standing. She wants to stay on her feet. Soon they hear people shouting for help. Now they know they're not alone—all the other elevators are stuck too.

To keep their minds off the situation, they talk to each other. Both of them worry—what are we going to do when we have to go to the bathroom?

Joyce and Sandy aren't the only ones in the dark. At 1:40 P.M. the lights go out all over the World Trade Center. To make sure there are no more fires or explosions, the electricity in all the buildings has been turned off.

On the fifty-eighth floor, engineer Eugene Fasullo can't see a thing either. He and his companions are still trapped in the elevator car. But they've almost broken through the wall. They seem so close to freedom. Without light, though, how can they keep digging?

Eugene is wearing a beeper. Other people are too. From each beeper shines a tiny ray of light. When they all hold the beepers up, they can make out the wall.

They keep working. The hole gets bigger and bigger. But smoke continually seeps in. Soon there'll be no air to breathe.

At last they break through the wall. Eugene

stares out the hole. The only thing he sees is…another wall! They have to keep digging.

In the packed elevator near the thirty-second floor, it's blacker than night and the school-children are frightened. The fifth graders quietly ask each other, "Are we going to die?"

A few of the adults flick their cigarette lighters. They burn like candles and cut into the darkness. The children cling to the adults, even the strangers.

One teacher has a cross on a string of beads with her. It's called a rosary. Some children hold on to it and pray. This rosary is special—it glows in the dark.

Unlike the classes in the elevator, the children on the tower roof have light. But now they have to go back into the building. They need to use the bathroom, so their teacher leads them indoors.

It's gloomy in the tower. There's no one around. The escalator isn't moving, so they have to walk down it. The wind comes howling in through the open roof door.

The children scream. The wind tears at their clothing. It shoots down the escalator and shoves them around. When they finally reach the bathroom, it's pitch-black.

More than fourteen hundred feet below, in the basement of the building, Kevin Shea's unit continues to hunt for him. They inch along the crater's edge and try to see through the thick smoke. They strain to hear a cry for help. They still don't know whether Kevin has survived.

Someone in the unit has an idea. Maybe Kevin is radioing for help, but the rubble is blocking his signals. A radio must be held where there can be no interference.

One of the firefighters lies down on the ground. The others grab his feet and dangle him upside down over the crater.

They hear Kevin! Soon they spot him by the fire's glow. They drop a rope down to him. But it's too short—he can't reach it. They lower a ladder—but it's not long enough either.

Meanwhile, other firefighters are searching through the basement. They find Joseph Cacciatore, his eye bleeding, his body soaking wet. It's a quarter to two when they get him upstairs.

Rescue workers also help John DiGiovanni, a forty-five-year-old salesman. He had just parked his car in the garage when the bomb exploded. They take him upstairs. He doesn't seem to be seriously hurt. But then something awful happens. He has a heart attack and dies.

Many people have been injured in the explosion. Hundreds are treated by Deputy Chief Paul Maniscalco. Some have broken bones, some have torn muscles. Others have cuts and bruises from flying glass or falling debris. There are people with asthma who are having trouble breathing.

But mostly people are sick from smoke inhalation. Smoke has prevented them from getting all the oxygen they need. Instead, they've been breathing the carbon monoxide in smoke. Carbon monoxide is a poisonous gas that can suffocate human beings.

Paul knows that smoke inhalation is a killer. It's the most common cause of death in a fire. The best way to prevent it is to stay low to the ground. That's because smoke always rises, along with heat. The safest way to escape a fire is to crawl to the nearest exit.

As people totter from the buildings, Paul and his fellow workers act quickly. They move together like a well-practiced team. Yet most of the rescuers have never met each other before.

Paul is proud they're so united. He thinks, "When the chips are down, people pull together." He believes New Yorkers are especially good at dealing with a crisis.

So many injured people come out of the towers that an emergency room is set up in Tower Two's lobby. Since there are no beds, stretchers are carried in. They won't fit through the revolv-

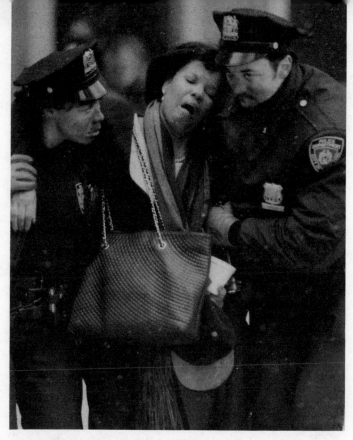

Two New York City police officers help a woman to safety. (AP/Wide World Photos)

ing lobby doors, so rescue workers bash in the door glass.

Rows and rows of stretchers cover the marble floor. On them people lie crying, or groaning from pain. Others are bleeding or curled up to get warm. Many have masks over their faces—they're breathing oxygen from tanks.

Those who aren't hurt volunteer to help. They use their own handkerchiefs to wipe blood from people's wounds. They sit by the injured, hold their hands, and give them water. Some go to pay telephones and call the victims' families.

Many of the injured are taken to the nearest hospitals. One hospital gets so crowded that patients are treated in the cafeteria. Another turns its gymnasium into an emergency room.

Agent Brenda Russillo knows she needs to get to a hospital. Shivering in her bare feet, she can't stop coughing. Her fellow Secret Service agents are having trouble breathing. Black mucus drips from their noses and shoots from their throats.

On the thirty-fourth floor, Geralyn Hearne is still sick. The firefighter who carried her there knows this pregnant woman needs a doctor. While her friend Donna tries to comfort her, he radios for medics. Two start up right away—but it won't be easy to reach her.

The medics are carrying one hundred pounds of equipment. They have to climb all the way to the thirty-fourth floor. As they head up the stairs, swarms of people pour downward. They're going to be fighting crowds with each step they take.

In just a few minutes, they're out of breath. Sweat drips down their bodies, and their legs feel as heavy as bricks. But they wouldn't think of giving up. They have lives to save.

Chapter 7

Gasping for Air

On the fortieth floor of the first tower, Jane Welsh is still struggling down the staircase. The smoke smells almost sweet and is as thick as fog. It is making her very thirsty.

Around her, people are wondering aloud whether the smoke contains poisonous chemicals. If it does, a few breaths might kill them all instantly. Should they go back? Jane wishes she'd see some firefighters. They would be able to tell her what to do.

She keeps trudging down. It gets harder to

breathe. By the twentieth floor, she can't see a thing. Now the smoke has lost its sweetness—it smells like burning rubber. She clutches the railing and thinks, "I may not make it out of here."

But ahead there's a beam of light! And a voice shouting instructions. It's a fireman with a flashlight helping the crowd. Now Jane knows she has a chance to make it to the street.

Lieutenant Dan Loeb turns his flashlight on and off. If he doesn't use it all the time, the batteries will last longer. He stands to one side of the staircase and directs people down. But it's getting so crowded, sometimes no one can move. Still, nobody panics. No one complains.

Because it's so dark, he tells everyone to grab the railing. He suggests counting stairs so people can figure out how far they've come. Over and over, he asks if anybody is disabled. He wants to make sure everyone gets the help they need.

Dan tells people to keep to the right. The left side of the staircase must stay open for emergencies. The crowd is cooperative. It's full of generous people. Some carry huge containers of water and offer drinks on the steps.

On another staircase, Arda Nazerian still fights to keep her balance. People are jammed together—it's like rush hour in the subway. Black smoke floats along the ceiling and washes over their heads.

Soon it's hot and hard to breathe. Arda wants to cover her mouth. That way soot and burning ash won't get into her lungs. She unfolds the collar of her turtleneck, stretching it over her mouth and nose. Other people unbutton their shirts and pull them over their faces.

But not everyone is trying to get out. Some people have decided to stay in their offices. They believe they'll be safest there.

Then smoke starts rolling in. It swells through the offices. It's like an unstoppable wave—it even spouts from the ceiling lights.

People don't know how to get away. They

*Office workers broke the windows of their smoke-filled
Twin Tower office to get fresh air.
(AP/Wide World Photos)*

can't decide what to do. Some get on the floor and wrap wet clothing around their faces. A few turn on battery-run televisions to watch the news for advice. Others use cellular phones to call TV stations for help. They hope the newscasters will let rescue workers know where they are.

The newscasters try to keep everyone calm. They suggest knocking through the ceilings of every office. The ceilings are made of tiles that can be pried off. When they're removed, each room will be taller. That way the smoke will have more space in which to rise, so the air near the floor will stay clearer longer.

But nothing seems to help some people. The smoke is like a heavy blanket they've gotten tangled up in. They feel they can't breathe. They believe they're going to die.

The newscasters tell people to break windows if they're desperate. The glass must be broken, since the windows don't open. On a number of floors, men and women grab coat racks and fire extinguishers. They swing them like bats through the panes. Then they stand by the jagged holes and suck in the fresh air. Some wave towels and coats to signal they're in trouble.

On the street below, a blizzard of glass comes pounding down. Rescue workers race to get people away from the towers. Inch-thick splinters sharp as knives fall toward the sidewalks. They're dropping at fifty miles per hour.

The rescue workers stand their ground. They won't desert the injured. It's a miracle no one is killed.

The firefighters worry about the broken windows. Now the smoke will travel faster. It will ride on the draft racing through the floors.

From the street, they stare up at the towers. Could this mean more people will die?

Chapter 8

Out of a Nightmare

All over New York City, people are talking about the World Trade Center. Everyone is asking what caused the explosion. Some turn on their TV's. Others listen to their radios. Right now it's hard to get any other news.

Many people have special reason to be anxious. Their friends and family work at the Trade Center. They won't move from their phones until their loved ones have called.

Those who are the most nervous are the parents of the schoolchildren. Nobody can tell them what's happened to their kids. They gather at the schools to wait together for any news. The principals and teachers come and join them.

In the elevator car, some of the children have fallen asleep. It's so hot inside—the temperature is in the nineties. A teacher strips off his shirt. The children take off coats and sweaters. One boy calls out, "I want my dad, I want my mom."

Everyone is thirsty, but there's nothing to drink. No one has anything but a few sticks of gum. They don't sing anymore, since that makes them even thirstier. Now there's nothing to do but sit and wait.

In another car, Eugene Fasullo and his comrades keep on digging. A smoky mist chokes them like hands around their throats.

On the stairs, Jane Welsh is gasping for breath. It's taking so long to get down. Three people are squeezed together on each step.

She's so thirsty. Her throat is sore. She thinks she's going to be sick, but she knows she has to keep moving.

Suddenly there's light. And fresh air! It's taken over an hour, but she's escaped from the tower!

Out on the street, she throws up. When she starts coughing again, someone offers her a peppermint.

Jane's face and hands are black. So is her red hair. Her coat used to be red too. Now it looks like it's been dipped in ink. Her glasses are still in place on top of her head. But she couldn't see out of them if she wanted—they're covered with greasy soot.

Right now Jane doesn't care. She's out of the nightmare, and she's safe. Her sore throat feels better after she has an ice cream cone. Now she'll head home to her family, crawl into bed, and watch TV.

But in the basement, the bad dream continues. Firefighters struggle to save Kevin Shea. They use a series of ladders to connect different levels of the rubble. Then they climb to the bottom of the crater. The descent is dangerous, since the rubble keeps shifting. There could be a cave-in at any minute.

But they make it! They're moving fast. They want to get out of this smoky hole. And they know Kevin is suffering terribly. They put him in a special stretcher with sides called a basket. It is handed from person to person along a human chain.

Kevin is roped into the basket. He can't fall out even if it turns upside down. The firefighters pass him along a path that zigzags up the crater. Every now and then, he's pulled by rope up a ladder.

Suddenly Kevin and the firefighters hear a shout. "Help!" a man cries. He must be the one Kevin was trying to rescue.

Where can he be? One firefighter thinks he

sees something stir. What is that sticking out of the rubble?

Slowly the thing moves back and forth. It looks as if it's waving. It's an arm! The man Kevin was searching for is buried alive.

The firefighters rescue Kevin and the man. They are both very lucky—they've survived.

Joseph Gibney feels lucky too, even if he is stuck on a staircase. Without his friends Jack and Andy, he wouldn't have gotten this far. He can't go down the stairs himself—no one in a wheelchair could.

But now Andy is too tired to help carry Joseph anymore. Jack can't do it himself. Then a stranger walks out of the darkness.

It doesn't seem to matter that they don't know one another. The stranger puts his arms around Joseph and helps Jack lift him up. As they inch down the stairs, the man shouts, "We're going to make it, we're going to make it."

All through the stairwells, people help one

another. Some start a relay system, shouting information from floor to floor. That way everyone will know what's happening. A man with a cellular phone calls 911 to ask what to do.

Pregnant women and the elderly are sent down the stairs first. If someone can't walk, people volunteer to carry them. One man carries a woman on his back from the 104th floor to the lobby.

People with asthma share their medicine with each other. People who have sodas give everyone a sip. People who have cough drops pass the package around—throats are burning from the smoke.

A few people pass out, but others stop and revive them. Some get exhausted and sit on the steps. No one gets angry, no one shoves them out of the way. If a rescue worker climbs by, there are shouts of "God bless you!"

Many are calm. They soothe those who are nervous. Some even crack jokes to relax the crowd. Arda Nazerian hears a voice say: "Here's a surefire way to get out early on a Friday."

The people on the stairs slowly climb down from the towers. By 3:00 P.M., thousands have escaped. They stumble out to the street, gasping for air. They look as if they've smeared their noses and mouths with dirt.

When Arda gets outside, she stares at herself in amazement. Her white tights and white sweater will never be clean again.

Michael Santoli can smell the smoke in his clothes. It's cold out on the street as he shares his clam chowder with a coworker. Finally he heads for home. Sometimes you just can't make a deadline.

But not everyone is so lucky. Many people are still trapped in the Trade Center. In the middle of the afternoon, smoke fills an elevator car. Ten people are stuck inside between the ninth and tenth floors. They lie down to keep the deadly vapor from their lungs. They wrap their coats

*Blast victims are given oxygen by emergency rescue crews
on the street outside the Trade Center.
(Dan Sheehan/Newsday)*

around their faces, then fling them over their heads.

But nothing works. They're coughing and choking. The smoke never stops coming—there seems to be an endless supply. It's as though they're stuck in a chimney, with a roaring blaze underneath.

Among the ten people, a husband and wife lie together, struggling to breathe. It's so dark they can't even see each other's faces. Only the sound of their voices tells them they are both there.

They have nowhere to go. There seems to be no escape. The couple admit to one another they think they're going to die. The other people in the car listen as they say good-bye to each other.

On Tower Two's roof, the schoolchildren shiver and shake. They huddle together to keep warm. Some of the children are so terrified their eyes are bulging out.

At last a few firefighters arrive. "Go back to

the observation deck," they tell the teachers. Much of the smoke has cleared away down there.

But the firefighters don't want the classes to go below the 107th floor. They think it's too early to start the long climb to the street. The staircases are still crowded, and the children might get hurt.

The teachers are worried. How much longer can their students hold out?

Chapter 9

The Great Escape

Inside the Trade Center, the elevators are still stuck. Joyce Reynolds and her friend Sandy are trapped in a motionless car. It's not silent, though—Sandy sings to keep herself calm.

Suddenly a voice comes out of nowhere. A man hollers, "You're next!" And the elevator starts rising.

At the third floor, the car jerks to a halt. The door opens slightly, and someone slips in a flashlight.

The police are outside! But they can't get the

door to budge. It takes another half-hour to pry it open.

Joyce staggers out. She hardly feels a thing. She leaves the building in a state of shock. In a little while, she bursts into tears. She's made it out alive. For five minutes she can't stop crying.

But Eugene Fasullo and his companions are still stuck. Right now, though, they're all feeling relieved. After three hours of digging, they've finally broken through both walls. And just in time—the smoke is suffocating.

In the dim light they can see beyond the second wall. The hole opens into a bathroom. To escape, they'll have to crawl into it. They must make the hole big enough to squeeze through.

They dig and claw. Finally the hole seems the right size. Most of them slip right through. But one man is heavier—he doesn't fit.

The man is stuffed into the hole. Gently they push and pull him. They know they can't use a lot of force because he could get stuck. He inches forward, he slithers and slides. All of a sudden, he bursts free!

At last they can make their way to safety. Fresh air and light await them fifty-eight flights down. But Eugene heads downstairs and reports to work! He must help repair the towers.

Not far away, the three Secret Service agents are in the hospital. For an hour and a half, all they can do is cough. Finally they start breathing normally, and the doctors say they can go home.

It's freezing outside, and Brenda still has no shoes. All she's got on her feet is a pair of green foam hospital slippers. The snow soaks right through them after a few steps outside. Later, one of her shoes is actually found in the garage.

Deborah Matut hasn't made it out yet. She's still on Tower One's roof. A helicopter whirs just above her, but it can't touch down. There isn't enough room on the roof.

Two policemen start to clear a space as big

as a landing pad. Every television antenna must be removed. All the roof lights have to be dismantled.

Deborah is praying the helicopter can land. It will pick her and six others up and fly them to the ground. To help the policemen, she tries to clear away the snow. She kicks at the drifts, then digs with her hands.

She can't stop thinking about her husband and her parents. If the helicopter can only reach her, she knows her life will be saved.

Finally the policemen finish. The helicopter drops close to the roof. There's a terrible wind and a deafening roar.

But the helicopter lands!

A group of repairmen pile out. They're here to fix the stalled elevators. Now passengers may board the helicopter. Deborah eagerly climbs on. At last she knows she's going to be all right.

Far below, on the forty-fourth floor, fireman Michael Dugan fears some other people might not have been so lucky. It's 3:30. The elevator door in front of him is tightly shut, and no one inside answers his calls. Whoever's sealed up in it has been trapped for over three hours.

Michael grabs his ax. He snatches up a metal bar. Other firefighters help him quickly pry the door open. Ten people lie inside, as still as corpses. It looks like a scene from a horror movie.

Suddenly there's a noise. A woman groans from under her coat. They're alive! The firefighters quickly radio for help.

Michael rushes into the car with his oxygen tank. These people may still be breathing, but they look just minutes away from death. The only thing that will save them is oxygen. Immediately.

Michael makes sure everyone gulps some air from the tank. In barely a minute, thirty rescue workers appear. They're determined to save these people.

Michael helps carry them out of the elevator.

Carefully they're removed, one by one. It takes two firefighters to carry each person. One holds the body under the armpits, the other under the knees. That way it's impossible for the person to fall. Slowly the unconscious people awaken. One man stirs and asks for his wife. A woman revives and whispers for her husband. It's the couple who thought they were going to die.

Michael can't believe what a close call they had. He can't help feeling he's part of a great rescue team. They've all worked together, in the true spirit of New York.

But there are still others to be saved. The schoolchildren are stifling in the elevator near the thirty-second floor. Some adults manage to pry the car door open a little. But thick black smoke comes billowing in along with the cool air. If help doesn't arrive soon, they're all going to suffocate.

Suddenly there's a bang! Someone's beating on the wall outside. The teachers boom out,

"We're in here, we're in here!" Lieutenant James Sherwood yells back, "We're going to get you out now." It's close to 4:30 P.M.—at last a firefighter has found them.

In order to free them, firefighters have to chop through the elevator ceiling. They use all their tools to hack out an opening. The children hear crashes and booms. Chunks of plaster and concrete hurtle into the car.

The teachers order the children to put their coats over their heads. No chunks smash into them, but one teacher gets smacked. A nasty bump quickly rises on her head.

The firefighters keep digging. Meanwhile, other children are moving toward the ground. The classes stuck on the 107th floor begin their walk down. Firefighters and policemen lead the way.

They beam their flashlights everywhere to make sure the children can see. They crack joke after joke, and all the kids laugh. They make the children relax and feel as if they're playing a game.

Around 4:30 P.M., they stop on the ninety-fourth floor. A firefighter takes the kindergartners into a large office where many people are waiting. Elise Constable has been there since the explosion.

She thinks the children are adorable. They plunk themselves down on the floor. Elise gets them soda and snacks. One little girl calmly tells her, "I thought I was going to die today."

Elise wants to comfort her. She says, "You don't think that now, do you?" She's relieved when the little girl answers no.

Soon the kindergartners leave. They continue their trek down. But the schoolchildren in the elevator are still waiting for rescue.

An hour has passed. The firefighters are still trying to reach them. Then, at about 5:30, a beam of light pierces the darkness. There's a hole in the car roof, and it's getting bigger by the second—the rescuers have arrived!

Lieutenant Sherwood looks down as the children reach up to him. "You are the bravest kids I've ever seen!" he shouts to them.

Kindergartners from Brooklyn's P.S. 95 elementary school are led from the towers after being trapped for five hours. (AP/Wide World Photos)

One by one, he begins to pull them out. Twelve children go up a ladder and are free. A parent who was with a class leaves too, to watch the children.

Suddenly the elevator jerks to life and begins to slip down the shaft. For an instant people wonder if it's falling.

But it descends smoothly and comes to a halt. When they look out the open door, the lobby is in front of them. They've been trapped almost six hours. Yet the school bus that brought them is still outside. The driver has waited all this time for them.

They smile and laugh. They're eager to go home. The afternoon in the elevator doesn't seem to have bothered them. But later, one boy speaks for all his classmates. He says, "I thought we were going to spend the night there for the rest of our lives."

At about the same time, Geralyn Hearne is rushed to a hospital. The medics can see she might die if they don't hurry. Her unborn baby is in danger too. Doctors will operate to try to save them both.

On this terrible day of destruction and despair, Geralyn Hearne gives birth to a little girl. She's tiny but healthy. Geralyn and her daughter are going to be fine.

A bomb has gone off and caused great tragedy. Yet as the day ends, a new life begins.

Chapter 10

When the Smoke Clears

It takes the whole night to evacuate the World Trade Center. Police check through the buildings until four the next morning. By the time the crisis is over, 1,042 people have been injured. That includes forty-four firefighters, one medic, and eleven police officers.

Six people die. The last one isn't found for seventeen days. Wilfredo Mercado was in his basement office when the bomb exploded. The floor collapsed, and he plummeted three stories to level B-4. Still sitting in his chair, he was buried under twelve feet of debris. Doctors believe he died instantly.

The Twin Towers are closed down for several weeks. Stores and companies in the Trade Center lose a billion dollars in business. A layer of soot covers desks, furniture, and walls. It takes thirteen hundred workers to clean and restore the buildings.

Almost immediately, an investigation into the explosion begins. New York's bomb squad arrives with eight specially trained dogs. The dogs have been taught to sniff out explosives. The squad can take a bomb apart in seconds.

The FBI is there, along with the police. A special government agency called the Bureau of Alcohol, Tobacco, and Firearms also sends agents. Together with the bomb squad, they confirm that a bomb has exploded. The World Trade Center has been the target of a terrorist attack.

But who did this terrible thing, and why?

Fifty-five different people make phone calls claiming responsibility. No one is quite sure whom to believe.

At first people believe the investigation will take months. They think the most important evidence is at the bottom of the crater. But it's not safe to go down there—debris is still falling. Engineers say it's possible that more of the basement will collapse.

Then late on Sunday, just two days after the explosion, ten experts head for the B-2 level of the garage. They carry flashlights and a camera. They also haul along kits to help them collect evidence. They're looking for clues right on the edge of the crater.

Agent Joe Hanlin peers carefully around. He's from the Bureau of Alcohol, Tobacco, and Firearms. Suddenly he spots a long, thin piece of metal. He can tell it's part of a truck or a van.

Joe gets excited. He knows the bomb was placed in a truck or a van. It had to have been too big and heavy to fit in a car. When the bomb exploded, it would have blown the truck or van to bits. Some of the bits would look just like this piece.

He turns the chunk over. He can't believe his luck. Stamped on the metal is part of a number. This number is called the VIN, or vehicle identification number. Every vehicle in the United States has one. When anybody buys a car, the owner's name and this number are registered with the government.

"Hey, look at this," he calls out to the team. If they can put the whole number together, they can find out what kind of vehicle it was. Even more important, they'll discover who owned it.

The agents sift through the rubble. More luck! They find other chunks of metal with numbers on them. Later one agent puts them all together. He enters the figure on an FBI computer—and the computer identifies it!

The vehicle that held the bomb was a yellow

Ford Econoline van. It was owned by a rental company located in New Jersey. The rental company tells the FBI the name of the man who leased it. Soon six men are arrested.

The men are Arabs from the Middle East. The police accuse them of belonging to a terrorist organization. The organization is called the Liberation Army, Fifth Battalion.

The Liberation Army claims it bombed the World Trade Center. It feels America has treated Arab countries unfairly.

The men who are arrested say they are innocent. The investigation continues. There are eight million pounds of rubble to comb through. The most important pieces are loaded into plastic bags. They're trucked to a place where they can be examined for clues.

People all over America are angry about the bombing. Innocent people have died, and many thousands have suffered. For weeks after the explosion, those who were there have night-

As the sun sets after a day of terror and confusion, the Twin Towers once again seem peaceful.
(AP/Wide World Photos)

mares. Some are frightened about returning to work. Others can think only about how they nearly died.

A number of experts believe the explosion could have been prevented. If more police were in the buildings, it would be harder to plant a bomb. They think the garage should now be closed to the public. As long as anyone can park there, terrorists can too.

They also feel the buildings need a new fire-safety system. No staircase exits should be locked, trapping people. The machines that control all the power to the buildings must be in an area totally separate from their backup systems.

One safety change has already been made—lights over the stairs are now battery operated. That way, if the electricity fails, people will still be able to see as they head down the steps.

But there's something else to learn from the World Trade Center bombing. Even when in danger, people can help each other. Though thousands were terrified, very few panicked. Many surprised themselves with their own courage.

These were ordinary people in an extraordinary situation. Few of them could have predicted how they would behave. Yet when disaster struck, it brought out the best in them. There were thousands of heroes on that terrible day.

One policeman said the bombing "didn't create terror." It had the opposite effect—"It bonded people together."

"There was so much goodness," Geralyn Hearne's friend Donna said. "There was goodness bigger than any bomb could be."

To Find Out More

Books

The Skyscraper Book by James Cross Giblin (Thomas Y. Crowell, 1981, 96 pages). Everything you would ever want to know about the tallest buildings in the world.

Skyscrapers: A Project Book by Anne and Scott MacGregor (Lothrop, Lee & Shepard, 1980, 56 pages). Shows how you can build your own model skyscraper and includes facts about the World Trade Center.

For junior high or high school readers, *Terrorism: Past, Present, Future* by Thomas Raynor

(Watts, 1987, 160 pages) gives an interesting account of terrorism through history.

Visit

You can visit the World Trade Center. The Observation Deck in Tower Two is open seven days a week until 9:30 p.m. For more information call (212) 435-7377. Many other skyscrapers have observation decks as well. Just call any building you are interested in visiting.

Acknowledgments

I want to thank those people who gave freely of their time and whose generous help made this book possible: Douglas Casper, Elise J. Constable, Michael Dugan, Timothy P. Farrell, Rose Kessler, Dan Leach, Dan Loeb, Marilyn Loeb, Paul M. Maniscalco, Deborah Matut, Arda Nazerian, Joyce Reynolds, Brenda Russillo, Michael Santoli, Kevin Shea, and Jane Welsh.

I am grateful to Tracy Devine, Amy Gross, Sarah Gross, Jo Irwin, Joy Johannessen, Joyce Kramer, Louis Kramer, Carol Leach, Dan Maynard of the Port Authority, Joseph Valiquette of the FBI, and Marian Whitaker, and to the Emergency Medical Service and the New York Police and Fire Departments, for their invaluable assistance and suggestions.

Last but not least I must give all due credit to the Random House editorial team for developing this project. It never would have happened without the imaginations, editorial dexterity, and interviewing skills of Judy Donnelly, Alice Jonaitis, and Regina Kahney, and the patience and persistence of Mike Novak.

Adrian Kerson

Index

Anderson, Donna, 19-20, 40, 55-56, 91

bomb, 7-11, 13-14, 15, 16, 17-20, 21-24
Bureau of Alcohol, Tobacco, and Firearms, U.S., 85, 86

Cacciatore, Joseph, 16-17, 34-35, 52
carbon monoxide, 53
children:
   in elevator, 24, 41, 50, 64, 78-82
   on roof, 41-42, 51, 71-72
Commodities Exchange, 18, 28, 47, 48
Constable, Elise, 80

DeLeo, Vito, 15-16, 34
DiGiovanni, John, 52
Dugan, Michael, 76-78

Emergency Medical Service (EMS), 30

Farrell, Timothy, 42-45
Fasullo, Eugene, 24-25, 49-50, 64, 74-75
Federal Bureau of Investigation, U.S., 11, 85, 87, 88
firefighters, 11-12, 26-28, 31-33, 51-52, 66-67, 76-78

garage, 6-9, 13-15, 29-30, 86, 90
Gibney, Joseph, 21, 40, 67

Hanlin, Joe, 86-87
Hearne, Geralyn, 19-20, 40, 55-56, 82-83
Hilton, Joann, 16, 34

Kessler, Rose, 17-18, 33
Kirkpatrick, Robert, 34
Knapp, Steven, 34

Leach, Dan, 18, 28-29
Liberation Army, 88
Loeb, Dan, 31-32, 58-59
Loeb, Marilyn, 33

Macko, William, 34
mall, 6, 17-18
Maniscalco, Paul, 30-31, 52-53
Matut, Deborah, 21-22, 45-46, 75-76
Mercado, Wilfredo, 84-85

Nazerian, Arda, 19, 35, 59, 69
New York Police Department, 33, 42, 76, 85

observation deck, 6, 41, 72
Red Cross, 11
Reynolds, Joyce, 18, 47, 73-74

95

Russillo, Brenda, 13-14, 29-30, 55

Santoli, Michael, 22, 39-40, 69
Secret Service, U.S., 6, 13
Shea, Kevin, 26-28, 37-39, 51-52, 66-67
Sherwood, James, 79, 80
Smith, Monica, 34

smoke inhalation, 52-53

train station, 6, 10

vehicle identification number (VIN), 87
Vista Hotel, 6, 10, 26, 33

Welsh, Jane, 23, 35, 57-58, 64-65